deep

feed

Phonics Friends

Eve's Green Garden
The Sound of Long E

The
**Child's
World**

By Cecilia Minden and Joanne Meier

seeds

weeds

The Child's World

Published in the United States of America
by The Child's World®
PO Box 326
Chanhassen, MN 55317-0326
800-599-READ
www.childsworld.com

The Child's World®: Mary Berendes, Publishing Director

Editorial Directions, Inc.: E. Russell Primm, Editorial
Director and Project Editor; Katie Marsico, Associate
Editor; Judith Shiffer, Associate Editor and School Media
Specialist; Linda S. Koutris, Photo Researcher and
Selector

The Design Lab: Kathleen Petelinsek, Design and Page
Production

Photographs ©: Corbis/Ariel Skelley: cover, 4; Corbis:
14, 20; Corbis/Michael Boys: 16; E. Russell Primm: 12;
Getty Images/Comstock: 6; Getty Images/ The Image
Bank/Tom Mareschal: 18; Getty Images/Photodisc
Gree/Ryan McVay: 8; Getty Images/Stone/Steve
Taylor: 10.

Library of Congress Cataloging-in-Publication Data
Minden, Cecilia.
  Eve's green garden : the sound of long E / by Cecilia
Minden and Joanne Meier.
    p. cm. — (Phonics friends)
  Summary: Simple text featuring the long "e" sound
describes how Eve plants and cares for a vegetable
garden.
  ISBN 1-59296-318-8 (library bound : alk. paper)
[1. English language—Phonetics. 2. Reading.] I. Meier,
Joanne D. II. Title. III. Series.
  PZ7.M6539Ev 2004
  [E]—dc22   2004002232

Note to parents and educators:

The Child's World® has created Phonics Friends with the goal of exposing children to engaging stories and pictures that assist in phonics development. The books in the series will help children learn the relationships between the letters of written language and the individual sounds of spoken language. This contact helps children learn to use these relationships to read and write words.

The books in this series follow a similar format. An introductory page, to be read by an adult, introduces the child to the phonics feature, or sound, that will be highlighted in the book. Read this page to the child, stressing the phonic feature. Help the student learn how to form the sound with her mouth. The Phonics Friends story and engaging photographs follow the introduction. At the end of the story, word lists categorize the feature words into their phonic element. Additional information on using these lists is on The Child's World® Web site listed at the top of this page.

Each book in this series has been carefully written to meet specific readability requirements. Close attention has been paid to elements such as word count, sentence length, and vocabulary. Readability formulas measure the ease with which the text can be read and understood. Each Phonics Friends book has been analyzed using the Spache readability formula. For more information on this formula, as well as the levels for each of the books in this series please visit The Child's World® Web site.

Reading research suggests that systematic phonics instruction can greatly improve students' word recognition, spelling, and comprehension skills. The Phonics Friends series assists in the teaching of phonics by providing students with important opportunities to apply their knowledge of phonics as they read words, sentences, and text.

The letter *e* makes two sounds.

The short sound of *e* sounds like *e* as in:
    egg and *hen*.

The long sound of *e* sounds like *e* as in:
    bee and *heel*.

In this book, you will read words that have the long *e* sound as in:
    deep, seeds, feeds, and *weeds*.

Eve is planting a garden.

She will grow vegetables.

Eve makes three rows.

She digs deep holes.

Eve puts seeds in the holes.

She covers the seeds with dirt.

The seeds will sleep in the earth.

Seeds need time to grow.

Eve feeds the seeds plant food.

Seeds need food to grow.

Eve waters the seeds.

Seeds need water to grow.

Soon the plants are growing.

Eve can see green plants.

Eve gets on her knees.

She needs to pull weeds.

Weeds keep plants

from growing.

Eve likes to be in the garden.

She likes to see green

plants grow.

Fun Facts

You might think that all seeds are tiny enough to fit inside the palm of your hand. This isn't true, however, for the seed of the double coconut palm tree. This seed can take 10 years to develop and has weighed in at more than 44 pounds (20 kilograms)! Double coconut palm trees are located on a chain of islands in the Indian Ocean.

Most people think weeds are annoying and try to keep them out of their gardens, but certain weeds can also be useful! Dandelions are a well-known weed. But, dandelion leaves are often used in salads, and the roots are sometimes an ingredient in a drink that is similar to coffee.

Activity

Planting Seeds in Your Garden
If you think you might make a good gardener, ask your parents if you can plant your own small garden in the backyard. Discuss what kinds of seeds you want to use and what time of year it is best to plant them. Once you have planted your seeds, be sure to water the garden regularly. Also pull any weeds that you see sprouting nearby. Keep a journal with pictures and notes describing how your plants are growing.

To Learn More

Books
About the Sound of Long E
Klingel, Cynthia, and Robert B. Noyed. *What a Week: The Sound of Long E.*
    Chanhassen, Minn.: The Child's World, 2000.

About Green Plants
Canizares, Susan. *Evergreens Are Green.* New York: Scholastic, 1998.
Halpern, Robert R. *Green Planet Rescue: Saving the Earth's Endangered
    Plants.* New York: Franklin Watts, 1993.

About Seeds
Anno, Mitsumasa. *Anno's Magic Seeds.* New York: Philomel Books, 1995.
Medearis, Angela Shelf, and Jill Dubin (illustrator). *Seeds Grow!.* New York:
    Scholastic, 1999.

About Weeds
Boyle, Constance. *Little Owl and the Weed.* Woodbury, N.Y.: Barron's
    Educational Books, 1985.

Web Sites
Visit our home page for lots of links about the Sound of Long E:

http://www.childsworld.com/links.html

Note to Parents, Teachers, and Librarians: We routinely check our Web links to make
sure they're safe, active sites—so encourage your readers to check them out!

Long E
Feature Words

Proper Names
Eve

Feature Words in Medial Position
deep
feed
keep
need
seed
weed

Feature Words in Final Position
be
knee
see
she

Feature Words with Blends and Digraphs
green
sleep
three

About the Authors

Cecilia Minden, PhD, directs the Language and Literacy Program at the Harvard Graduate School of Education. She is a reading specialist with classroom and administrative experience in grades K–12. She earned her PhD in reading education from the University of Virginia. Cecilia and her husband Dave Cupp enjoy sharing their love of reading with their granddaughter Chelsea.

Joanne Meier, PhD, has worked as an elementary school teacher and university professor. She earned her BA in early childhood education from the University of South Carolina, and her MEd and PhD in education from the University of Virginia. She currently works as a literacy consultant for schools and private organizations. Joanne Meier lives with her husband Eric, and spends most of her time chasing her two daughters, Kella and Erin, and her two cats, Sam and Gilly, in Charlottesville, Virginia.